D1398752

My Chameleon Teacher

To Joey and Gianna,
I hope you enjoy my true story.
May it encourage and inspire you.
Love,   Kim Davis

Published and distributed by Merack Publishing.

Library of Congress Control Number: 2020919590

Davis, Kim,

My Chameleon Teacher

Illustrated by Lesia Klymenko

ISBN Paperback 978-1-949635-66-9, Hardcover 978-1-949635-67-6

My Chameleon Teacher

Written by Kim Davis

Illustrated by Lesia Klymenko

MERACK

This book is dedicated to my family and friends near and far, thank you for always praying and supporting me. Also, Stephanie, my friend and team teacher, who encouraged me to write my story about our 4th grade students during the school year of 2018-2019 from room 407.

Every teacher I've ever had has been kind of the same. You know: they're kind and smart, usually funny, but some can be so strict. From what I hear, Mrs. Davis is all these things and more. My name is James, and I hear I lucked out and got a "good one" this year (even though she's sorta old.)

I knew fourth grade was going to be great just by the way our teacher had us get to know each other. We started this morning with a get to know you game. Mrs. Davis sorted us by birthdays, the number in our families, and the color of our hair. She said, "Everyone with blonde hair, stand in the front corner. Brown hair, go to the back corner. All other colors, stay in the middle." I had blonde hair! I went to the front and so did Mrs. Davis. That's when I noticed her hair was like my mom's—shoulder length and blonde.

Routine is what our classroom ran on, so every morning we had a meeting where Mrs. Davis wrote us a letter about what was up for the day. I guess some of our classmates need structure. Not me—I'm a go with the flow kinda guy, not always paying attention to what's going on around me. What I did notice is that towards the end of September Mrs. Davis seemed tired and not her perky self. And if you ask me, her hair looked a little different everyday.

October entered with a chilly fall breeze, and... you won't believe it... Mrs. Davis came to school with LONG HAIR! Wait a minute! Something is going on, but what?

My first thought was MAGIC, but my friend Frankie pointed out to me that magic isn't real. I reluctantly agreed, but no matter what, my teacher was changing right in front of me. Not only was her hair changing, but her eyes were like an x-ray machine!

She could see some of us sneaking behind her back not doing what we were supposed to be doing. I'll admit it, I was one of those kids that got busted a few times, but she also saw the kids that did good things too. Even Nik, who really had a hard time with his schoolwork, usually avoiding tasks, caught Mrs. Davis' attention and she somehow always got him to do his best. I don't care what Frankie says, that's MAGIC!

Then came the best Friday of the year: Favorite Sports Team Day. I headed down the fourth grade hallway, and was so excited to see everyone's gear. We all knew who Mrs. Davis' favorite team was... would she be decked out too?

"Good Morning James," said Mrs. Davis cheerfully.

"Good Morning Mrs. Davis," I st-t-tuttered back, barely able to speak.

Mrs. Davis, once again, looked totally different. Her hair was PINK, SUPER LONG, and pulled back in a ponytail underneath a baseball cap that matched her jersey. She looked really hip, and a lot younger with that ponytail! I tried not to stare, but couldn't help myself. You could tell everyone else knew something was up, because we all had the same look on our faces (you know, the one where your mouth is wide open and your eyes don't seem to blink?)

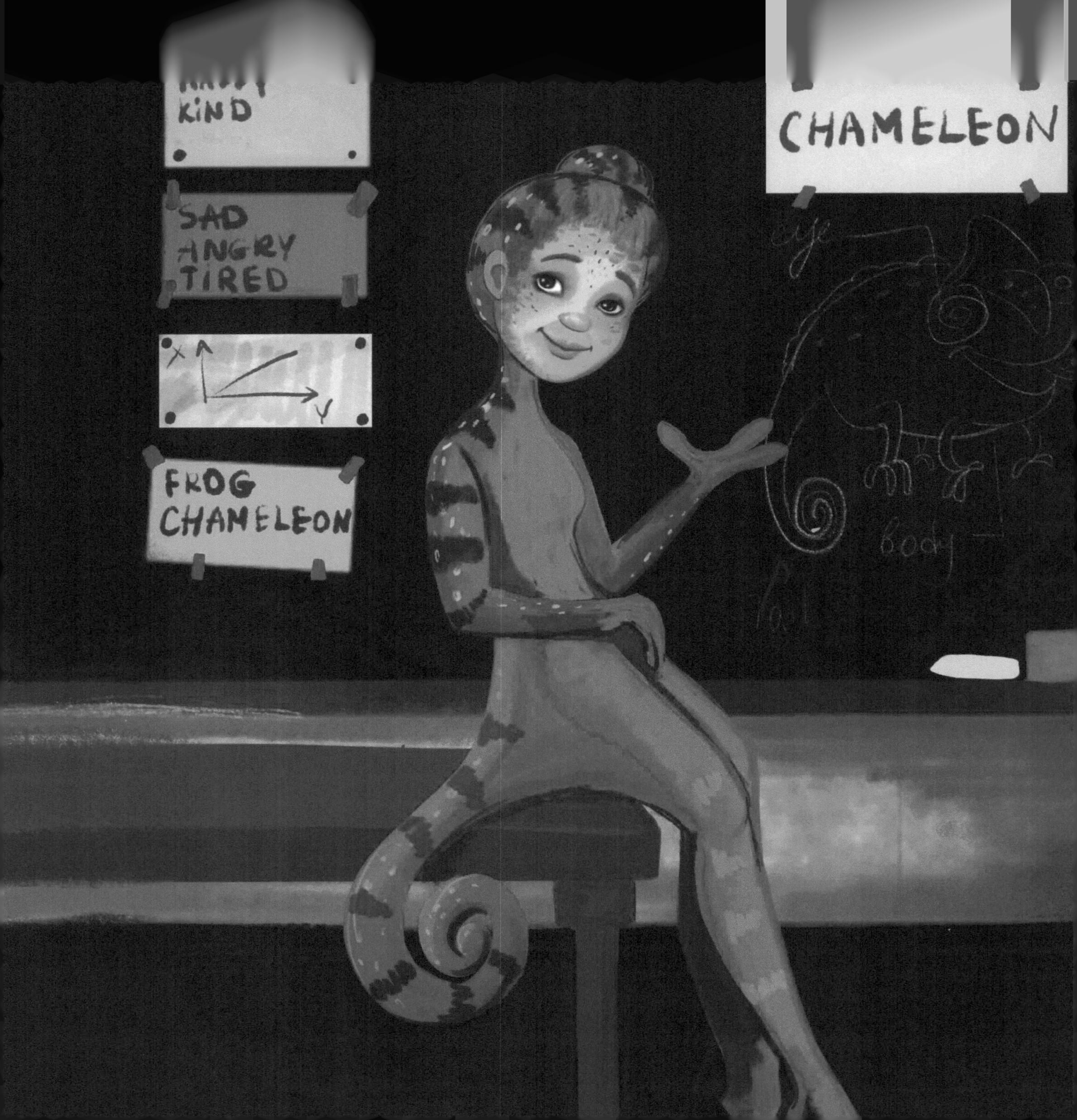
KIND
SAD
ANGRY
TIRED
x
y
FROG
CHAMELEON
CHAMELEON
eye
body

I started to think she was like a chameleon. You see, chameleons can change their appearance by color and mood to match their environment, and I was beginning to think my teacher could do the same. I wondered to myself, did anyone else see her this way, or was it just me? I couldn't figure out the mystery behind her.

Or was it just me?

As I slid into my chair, there was a ton of chatter.
Erin was whispering to Emily, "Did you see Mrs. Davis'
long hair?"

Landon, with his hands cupped over his mouth, was at the cubbie he shared with Dillon snickering at something. You could hear the whispers around the room like crickets on a quiet night.

At today's morning meeting, all you could see of the daily letter to our class was just the greeting. I wondered why the rest was covered up. Mrs. Davis must have something exciting under there to share with us today.

She always started the letter with a cheerful type of Good Morning greeting, but today she paused, took a deep breath in through her nose, held it for a second, and let it out. This was unusual, it wasn't like any other morning. Instead of reading from the screen where she usually projected the daily letter she held a letter in her hand.

Our teacher almost looked frightened. As she began to read the letter aloud, her voice shook, just a little. She had told us she was working on a story and wanted to share it with us. As I looked around I could see everyone's eyes looking straight ahead, like a movie had just started.

Mrs. Davis first started to tell us that she had heard rumblings over the past few weeks, whispers here and there. She also said, "I've watched your faces when you've seen my new 'looks' so I want to share something I've been going through for the last several months. This year I've decided to be like a chameleon."

"Chameleon, I guessed it!" I whispered under my breath as Mrs. Davis continued talking.

It was about to get even MORE crazy. As she slowly removed her hair, she told us her different looks were wigs, and the reason she wore them is because she is battling CANCER.

There it was.

Her looks! It was all coming together now. Mrs. Davis has cancer! My teacher has cancer! Not a peep out of anyone, not a squirm or a wiggle on the carpet. No one made a noise, not even Sofia (and if you knew Sofia, that's pretty amazing.)

As we sat on the rug, my mind started thinking of what I knew about cancer. Everyone had heard of cancer, including me, but I realized I didn't actually know much about it besides feeling like it was not a good thing. My heart began to race with worried thoughts.

Mrs. Davis started to tell us what she was going through. She was tired some days, and not always feeling her best. She was taking medicine to help her fight her battle with cancer, which is why she had lost her hair. When she removed her wig she didn't want to frighten us, but wanted us to know what it was really like. You could feel the sympathy in the room.

We had lots of questions and Mrs. Davis calmly answered each and every one of them. Landon asked, "What does it feel like to not have hair?" and then Dillon raised his hand and asked, "Will your hair grow back?"

"It feels kind of funny, actually a little stubbly, and yes it will eventually grow back once I'm finished taking the medicine." replied Mrs. Davis.

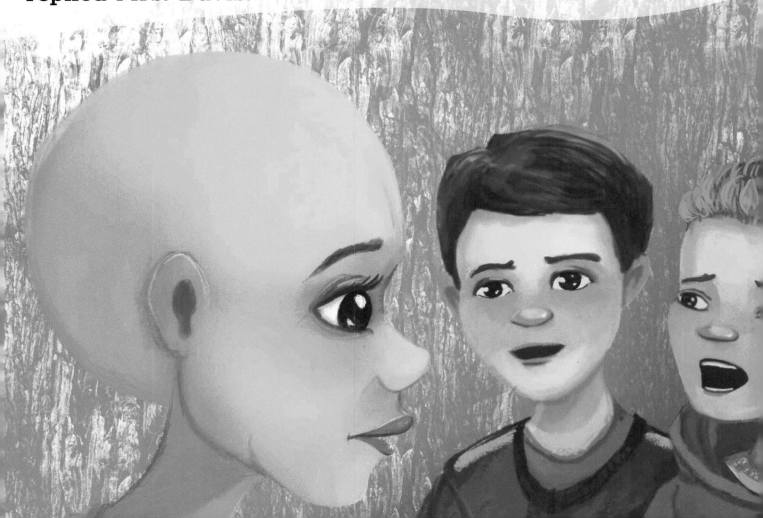

hen Emily asked what we were all wondering, "Will you be
ere the whole school year?" Emily is the smarty pants of our
ass, so of course she was thinking ahead.
Yes, I'm going to try my best," which is what Mrs. Davis
ways expected of us. "But in the meantime, you better be
eady, you never know which teacher you're going to recognize
ach day. Long hair, short, hair, blonde hair, pink hair... a
hameleon, remember?" she said with a smile on her face.

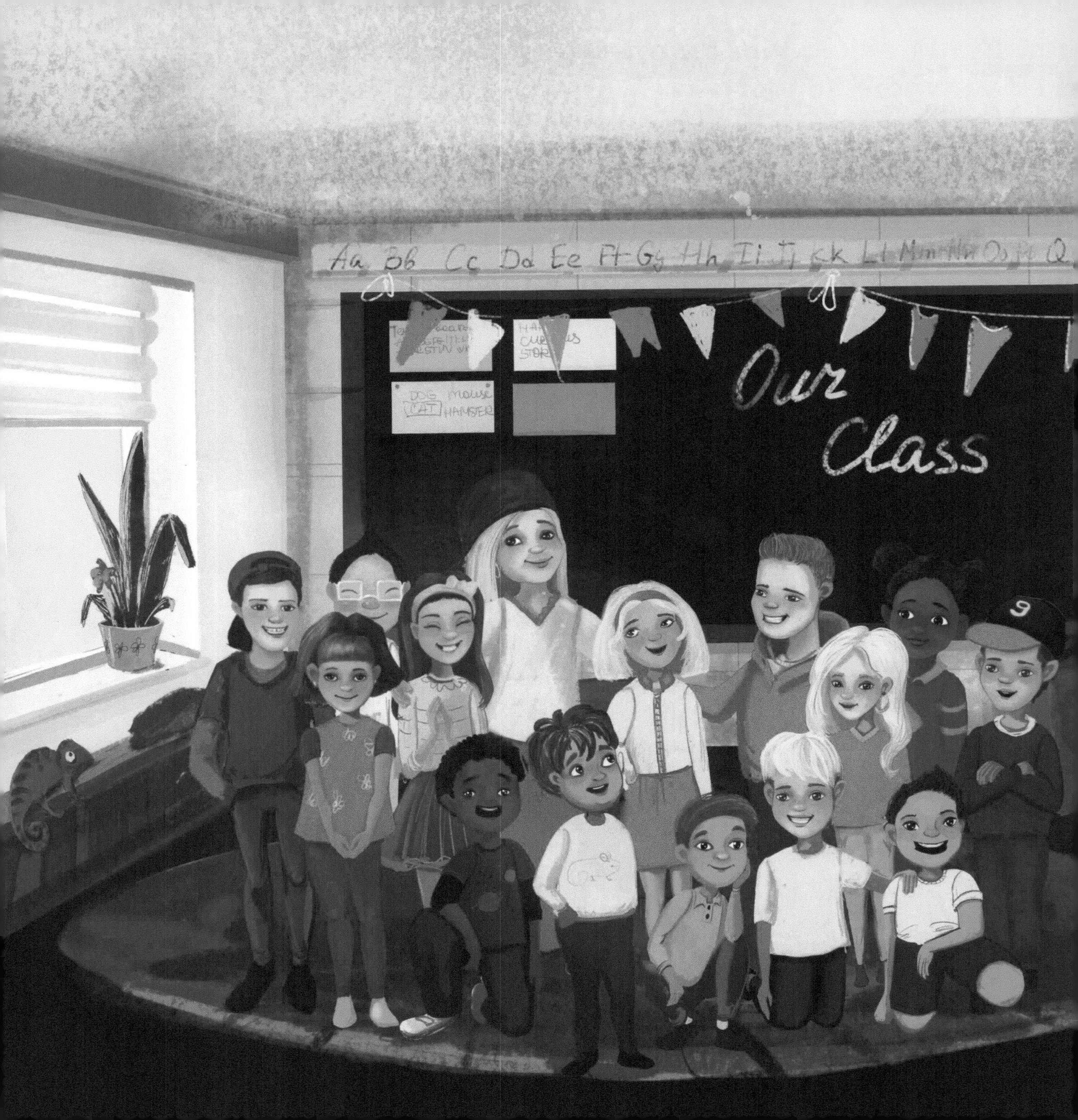
Our Class
DOG mouse
CAT HAMSTER

As the year went on, we all stepped up when we knew she was having one of those days. It's like we became a team that year, always cheering, always applauding, always there for each other no matter what the day brought.

That 4th grade year was one of my best years in all of my school memories. Mrs. Davis' strength and courage taught us all many life lessons—things we would never learn from a book.

Our class learned to be compassionate when others are going through a tough time. We learned that when a hurdle comes our way we can hop over it and keep going (like Nik in our class always had to, because school wasn't easy for him.) Our class motto, and Mrs. Davis' favorite saying was, "Be kind to one another." And we were.

stay positive

be strong

stand up for yourself

be kind

Our chameleon teacher kept us guessing: one day short hair, the next day long, never knowing what we were going to get. But that didn't matter to us. What mattered was we had a teacher who showed us how to be brave. To keep going and stay positive. To stand up for ourselves. To be kind above all else. And when life is hard sometimes, DON'T EVER GIVE UP!

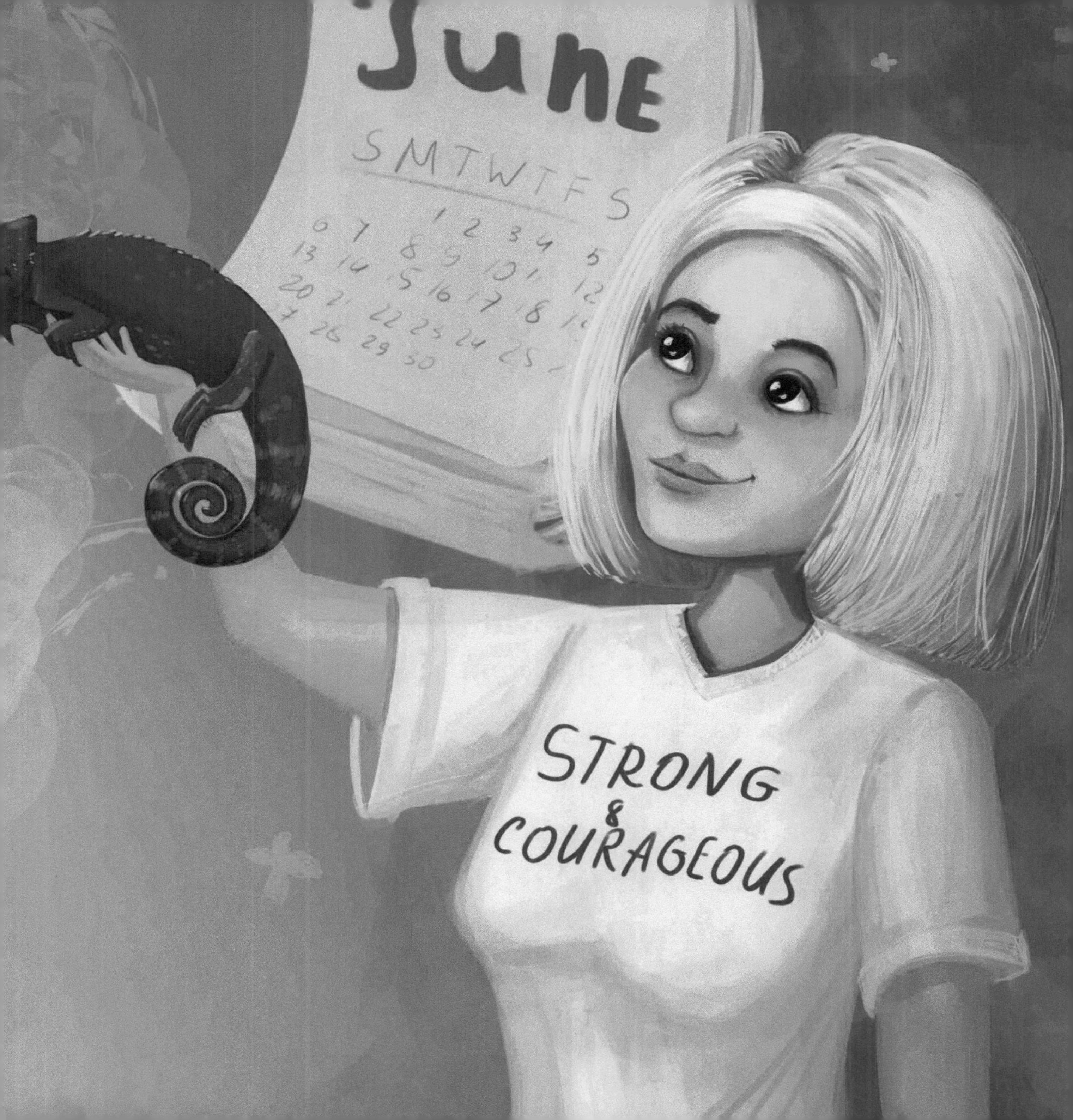
June
S M T W T F S
STRONG
&
COURAGEOUS

ABOUT THE AUTHOR

As a first time author, Kim Davis, began writing her book while battling a rare Sarcoma cancer. She was diagnosed in the middle of the school year in 2017. Her inspiration to write this story sparked from her students and how they handled knowing their teacher had cancer and continued to teach through surgeries and treatments. Her strength comes from her faith, and only through God's grace she was able to write this book. She lives with her husband, Scot, and has two sons, Landon, and Dillon. They are the loves of her life and couldn't do this journey without them. She is originally from Ohio where her extended family still remains, and hopes to someday move back there. For now, New Jersey remains her home, where she is currently undergoing treatment while writing this story.

CPSIA information can be obtained
at www.ICGtesting.com
Printed in the USA
LVHW070011101120
671122LV00019B/662